READ.
SHARE.
REPEAT.

A Gift For

Mrs. Hayward

From

Meagan Hughes

■SCHOLASTIC

W9-CDF-200

This book belongs to:

....

....

....

For my godchildren Sarah,
Jack, and Tess - FT

For our Elinor, who lives life in a
whoosh and a whirl! Love, MMC

Text copyright © 2010 by Fiona Tierney
Illustrations copyright © 2010 by Margaret Chamberlain

All rights reserved. Published by Chicken House, an imprint of Scholastic Inc.,
Publishers since 1920. First published in the United Kingdom by Chicken House, 2 Palmer Street, Frome, Somerset
BA11 1DS. www.doublecluck.com CHICKEN HOUSE, SCHOLASTIC, and associated logos are trademarks and/or registered
trademarks of Scholastic Inc. www.scholastic.com

Library of Congress Cataloging-in-Publication Data
Tierney, Fiona.
Lion's lunch? / by Fiona Tierney ; illustrated by Margaret Chamberlain. · p. cm.
Summary: When Lion comes upon Sarah walking in the jungle, he threatens to eat her unless she shows that she can do something that none of the other animals can do.

ISBN-13: 978-0-545-17691-0 · ISBN-10: 0-545-17691-3

[1. Lions—Fiction. 2. Animals—Fiction. 3. Jungles—Fiction. 4. Drawing—Fiction.] I. Chamberlain, Margaret, ill. II. Title.
PZ7.T442Li 2010 · [E]—dc22

2009008267

10 9 8 7 6 5 4 3 2 1   10 11 12 13 14

Printed in China · First American edition, January 2010
Text was set in HenHouse. Book design by Whitney Lyle

Lion's Lunch?

By Fiona Tierney

Illustrated by
Margaret Chamberlain

Chicken House

Scholastic Inc. / New York

Sarah was walking through the jungle, singing happily, when a big lion pounced from behind a bush. **"What are you doing in my jungle?"** he roared.

"P-please, Mr. Lion," whispered Sarah. "I was only going for a walk."

swoop

lumber

prowl

gallop

flit

"A WALK! Nobody here just walks.
We run, sprint, prowl, creep, swing,
lumber, slither, swoop, gallop,
and scuttle. YOU shouldn't be here,
this is my jungle."

"I'm sorry, I didn't mean
to bother you," said Sarah.

"And what was that
sound?" snapped Lion.

"I was s-singing,"
said Sarah.

"**SINGING!** Nobody here just **sings.**
We roar, yowl, grunt, chatter, buzz, trumpet,
hiss, growl, pant, and harrumph."

grunt

oink

hiss

ROAR

grunt

croak

"I'm sorry,"
said Sarah.
"I didn't mean
to bother you."

"Since you shouldn't be here,
I'm going to eat you," said Lion.

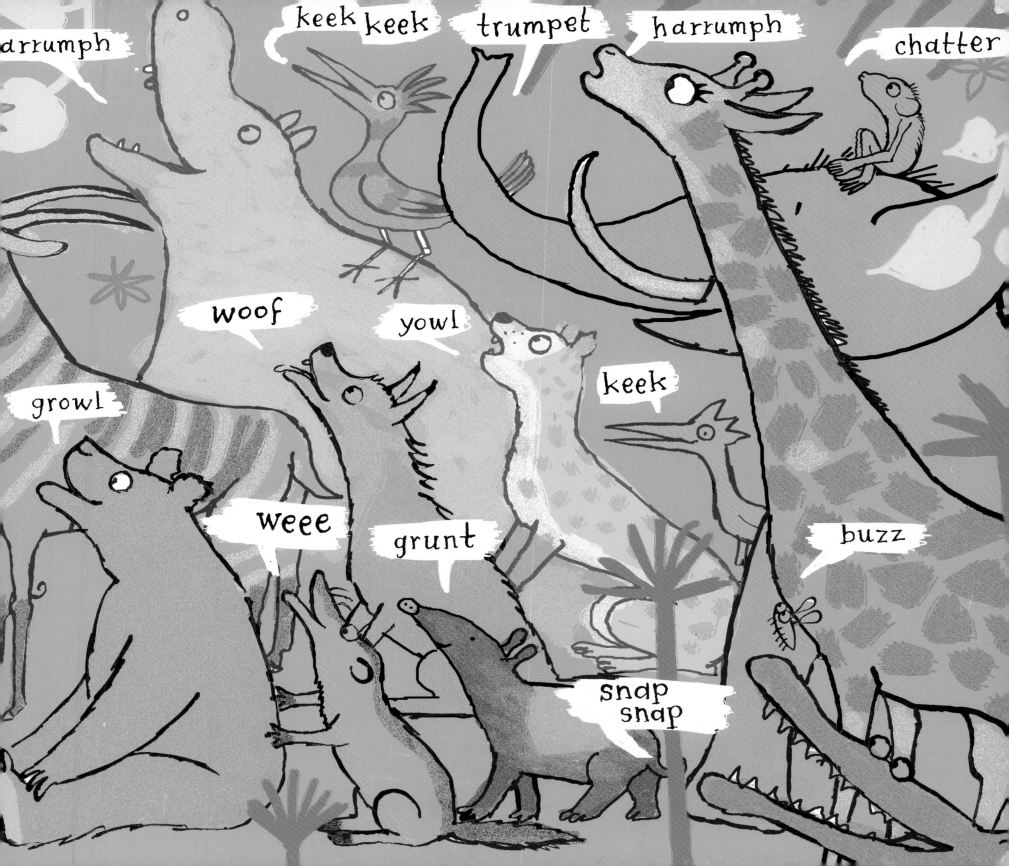

"Please don't eat me,"
pleaded Sarah.
"I love the jungle.
Tell me what
I can do to stay."

"Let me see," jeered Lion, ticking off his sharp **claws** one by one.

"You can't run like Cheetah
or climb like Monkey
or swim like Crocodile
or stalk like Tiger
or leap like Gazelle
or hide like Chameleon
or reach like Giraffe
or wallow like Hippopotamus
or float like Butterfly
or wriggle like Snake.

"Now **I'm** out of claws, and it looks to me like **you're LUNCH!**"

Lion licked his lips
and got ready to **leap.**

"Wait!" said Sarah.
"If I can do something

that nobody else in the jungle

can do, will you

let me stay?"

"What can **you** possibly do that we can't do **better?**" asked Lion.

"**I can draw,**" said Sarah.

"Draw!" said Lion. "What can you draw?"

"You!" replied Sarah. She took out her paper, pencils, and paints. "Because you are King of the Jungle."

As she drew, the other animals gathered behind her.

"Finished," said Sarah at last, and she showed Lion her picture.

Lion looked.

Lion saw . . .

A Great Big Angry Lion!

"That's not **me**," he growled.
"I'm handsome, but you've made me look mad and mean.
I will eat you because you **can't** draw."

"**OH YES SHE CAN,**" chorused the other animals. "You're bad-tempered and bossy. Let her draw us and you'll see."

So, while Lion sulked, Sarah drew all the other animals.

Friendly Squirre

Jazzy Snake

Cuddly Bear

Pretty Leopard

Perky Porcupine

Sleepy Stork

Snappy Crocodile

"See!" said the animals. "Sarah only draws it like it is."

Lion looked at his picture and the other drawings. Then he looked at Sarah and the other animals. "Sarah, you are free," he said in a voice that was quiet and thoughtful. "It's getting late. Let me walk you safely out of the jungle."

"NO," said the other animals. "You are too grumpy and bossy. We will go with Sarah."

And they all set off in a merry, noisy, happy bunch,
with Lion following far behind.

When everybody had said good-bye,
Lion came up to her and said,
"I don't like the way I look.
Sarah, I wish I could change."

"You are a big, strong, and wonderful lion,"
said Sarah.
"Maybe you could try helping everybody
instead of bullying them. I'm sure that will
change the way you look!"

"Please come back and draw me again. You'll see
a difference, I promise," said Lion.

"I'll come again next month,"
said Sarah.

And guess what she drew next time?

A Great Big Happy Lion!

Lion smiled when he saw the
new picture.
"Thank you, Sarah," he said.

"You are welcome to walk and sing and draw in **OUR** jungle whenever you like!"